Clifford's puppy days

PUPPY LOVE

By Lisa Ann Marsoli

Based on the Scholastic book series "Clifford The Big Red Dog" © Norman Bridwell

Illustrated by Jim Durk

ISBN 0-439-61116-4

18 17 16 15 14 13 12 11   08 09 10 11 12/0

Design by Peter Koblish

Printed in the U.S.A.   First printing, January 2004

SCHOLASTIC INC.
New York   Toronto   London   Auckland   Sydney
Mexico City   New Delhi   Hong Kong   Buenos Aires

Before Clifford was a Big Red Dog, he was a small red puppy.
He lived with Emily Elizabeth and her family in an apartment in the city.

Everyone loved Clifford. They were always telling him so.
"I love you," said Emily Elizabeth when she tickled Clifford's tummy.

"I love you," said Mrs. Howard when
Clifford climbed up in her lap.

"Yes, I love you, too!" Mr. Howard told Clifford when the puppy greeted him at the door.

Clifford didn't know what the word "love"
meant, exactly.
He liked the way his family's voices sounded
when they said it, though.

Clifford's friends talked about love, too.
"I love it when we play!" said Clifford's friend Jorge.

The dachshund's tail wagged with happiness.

"We love coming to visit," said Flo. "You're lots of fun!"

"And you're it!" Zo added. She raced down
the hall while Clifford tried to tag her.

"I love it when we eat together," Daffodil said. "It's nice to have a friend to keep me company."

"We love talking to you, Clifford," said the youngest mouse in the Sidarsky family.

"You're a good listener."

Clifford was confused. Love seemed to mean
an awful lot of things!
Maybe Norville could explain it.

"What is love?" said Norville. "That's easy. It's when someone gives you a bowl full of your favorite birdseed!"

Clifford was more confused than ever.
He didn't even like birdseed!

One summer night, Emily Elizabeth and Clifford sat on the steps sharing an ice-cream cone. The sunset was pretty and pink. The breeze was nice and warm.

"I love you, Clifford," said Emily Elizabeth as she scratched him behind the ears.

Suddenly Clifford understood! Love was the warm, happy feeling you got when you were with someone you cared about.

Clifford sighed with contentment. "I love you, too, Emily Elizabeth," he thought.